PETER and FRIENDS
Sticker Activity Book

Do the activities to win your puzzle skills award!

Want to go on an adventure?

Come on . . . let's hop to it!

D1223840

Can you spot a yummy **radish** in every activity?

CATCH ME IF YOU CAN!

Mr. McGregor has such juicy radishes in his garden. Uh-oh, **here he comes!** Can you find a way out of the garden?

START

Wrong way!
Mr. Tod wants us for dinner.

Go back!
Mr. McGregor
has spotted us.

FINISH ▶ Made it!
Add a sticker of my
mother waiting for
us at home.

BEST FRIENDS COLOR CLUES

Peter Rabbit is my **best** friend. Find a sticker to match the outline, then use it to help you color in the big picture.

NUTTY JIGSAW JUMBLE

Those silly squirrels have lost **three** pieces from this jigsaw! Find the right stickers to finish the picture. **Let's go!**

WATCH OUT FOR THE FOX

You never know **who** you might run into . . .
Find stickers to match these shadows, and if we
see Mr. Tod it's time to get out of here, **fast!**

She's small and cute—
my baby sister.

Well, ruffle my feathers!
She's always in a flap.

This sneaky fox wants
rabbit pie for supper!

This soggy froggy
loves fishing.

She has lots of prickles,
but she's a real softy.

THERE GOES MY TUMMY ALARM!

Rabbits are brave and we **love** exploring! One of these trails leads to a **yummy** strawberry. Can you find the right path?

Add a strawberry sticker when you find the path. Yum!

TREEHOUSE ADVENTURE

Welcome to the sky-high Squirrel Camp! Use your stickers to make up amazing adventures for us. Ready? Let's do it!

JUST-IN-CASE POCKET

My magnifying glass is **perfect** for finding clues—I know that for a fact! Draw more things we might need . . . just in case.

A GOOD RABBIT NEVER GIVES UP

These pictures look the same, but **six** things are different in the second picture. Put a tip-top spotter sticker on each one you find.

I-SPY WHO'S WHO

Psst! Let's play I Spy. Who can you see? When you've figured out who's hiding, put the right stickers in each circle.

13

LIFE IS ONE BIG ADVENTURE

We're on an important mission . . . Play this game with a friend to help us get through the woods safely.

Let's hop to it!

START

1 2 3 4 5 6

Help Mrs. Tiggy-winkle with her washing. Miss a turn.

21 20 19

22

23 Find a secret escape tunnel. Go forward 2 spaces.

24 25 26 Mr. Tod chases you. Go back 2 spaces.

First find a die. Then fold the special stickers to make your game pieces. Now take turns to roll the die and move the right number of spaces.

7 Hear a strange noise and go to investigate. Miss a turn.

8

9

10

11 Find a secret escape tunnel. Go forward 3 spaces.

12

13

14

15 Benjamin is scared! Miss a turn.

16

17 Spot a radish trail. Go forward 2 spaces.

FINISH

You're the winner! Collect your medal sticker.

30

29

27

28 Squirrel Nutkin tells a funny story. Go back 1 space.

You've finished!
That's brilliant!

CONGRATULATIONS!
PUZZLE SKILLS CERTIFICATE
Awarded to

_____

_____

Age

_____

Peter Rabbit
_____

PETER RABBIT
CHIEF ADVENTURER

ANSWERS

Pages 2–3

Page 5

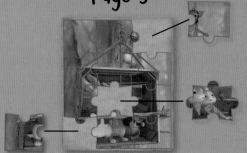

Page 6

Page 7
It's path C

Page 11

Pages 12–13